Family Storybook Library

# Nothing Is Stronger
# Than a Parent's Love

## Stories About Family

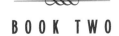

BOOK TWO

First Edition
1 3 5 7 9 10 8 6 4 2

ISBN: 0-7868-5867-2

# Nothing Is Stronger Than a Parent's Love

———∞∞∞———

## Stories About Family

# Introduction

Unconditional parental love is the greatest gift that we can give to our children. The knowledge that we love and respect them despite their mistakes is a tremendous comfort to children. Knowing that they can call on us for help and support is an invaluable resource for them.

Attractive as Never Land is to Wendy, Michael, and John, the lure of home and the steadfast love their parents provide is overpowering. King Triton may live under the sea, but his selfless act of love for Ariel is one that any parent can understand.

# Home, Sweet Home

from *Peter Pan*

*There's no better way to end the day
than with a kiss from Mom or Dad.*

The Darling children had heard many wonderful stories about Peter Pan, but they never dreamed they would ever really meet him. So when Peter Pan flew into the nursery one night, they were delighted.

"Come with me to Never Land," Peter told Wendy, John, and Michael. And so they did, flying through the night sky with him and his pixie friend, Tinker Bell.

Never Land was filled with all sorts of interesting people. The Lost Boys were

Peter Pan's friends, and they were very excited that he had brought some new children to play with them.

"This is Wendy," Peter Pan explained. "And I've brought her here to be your mother."

Wendy shook her head. "I can't be their mother," she explained. "I still need my own mother too much."

None of the Lost Boys had mothers of their own anymore. "What's a mother?" one of the Lost Boys asked Wendy.

Wendy felt very sorry for them. "She's a wonderful person who loves you very much," Wendy told them.

Peter Pan frowned. The Lost Boys seemed more interested in mothers than in playing pirates.

Wendy went on. "A mother tells you wonderful stories and kisses you good night at the end of the day."

"Are you our mother?" Michael asked Wendy.

"Of course not," Wendy said. "I'm your sister. Don't you remember our real mother?"

John picked up his hat. "I remember her, Wendy!" he cried.

"And I propose we go home to her at once!"

Wendy, John, and Michael said good-bye to Peter Pan and his friends. Never Land grew smaller and smaller as they flew through the sky toward home, where their own mother was just getting ready to kiss them all good night.

# King Triton's Gift

from *The Little Mermaid*

———⦿———

*A loving father cannot help but forgive.*

King Triton was exuberant. Together, he and Eric had defeated the wicked sea witch, Ursula, and saved the merpeople from her evil schemes. But before he could rejoice, he had to find Ariel. He knew that his daughter would not be happy until she was rejoined with her true love.

Triton hadn't approved of Eric, or of any humans, for that matter. He had seen too many sea creatures snagged by their cruel fisheaters' hooks. But now he realized that

Eric was different. Eric had risked his own life to save Ariel—and for that, Triton would always be grateful.

Sebastian and Flounder led the Sea King to the shore where Ariel was sitting on a rock. She was mournfully watching Eric as he lay unconscious on the sand.

Triton turned to Sebastian. "She really does love him, doesn't she?"

"Mmm." Sebastian agreed.

"Well then, I guess there's just one problem left," mused the King.

"What's that, Your Majesty?"

"How much I'm going to miss her." Sebastian's jaw fell open. With a sigh, Triton raised his trident and sent a beam of magical light toward Ariel.

As Ariel looked down to see what was

happening, she saw her fish tail being transformed into legs—human legs like she had always dreamed of! She looked up and beamed at her father.

Eric began to stir. When he saw Ariel walking toward him out of the ocean, his face lit up. At last they were free! And they

belonged to
each other.

King Triton
smiled sadly.
He knew that
he would not
be able to see
his remarkable
daughter every
day as he had
in the past. But
he was warmed
by the knowledge
that she would
have a happy
future with a man
who loved her as
much as he did.